MW00909588

In honor of my Dad-
who after my endless begging,
finally let us get a dog.

Along a small road
in a house on the hill,
there lived a dog, Bailey,
the dog with no chill.

The Dog with No Chill

Written by Elise Mariolis

Illustrated by George Franco & Elise Mariolis

Copyright © 2020 by Kitten Kaboodle Publishing

All rights reserved. No part of this book may be
reproduced or used in any manner without written
permission of the copyright owners, with the exception of
that covered under fair use.

She'd whine to come in, and she'd whine to go out,
and she'd whine when she itched
at the end of her snout.

She'd whine cause her toy
was high up on the shelf,

"I was meant to be a big dog,"
she'd say to herself.

She'd whine to be played with, and whine to be fed, and whine cause she couldn't get up on the bed.

She would bark when it's dark
and would gripe when it's light.

She would howl all day,
and then whimper all night.

She'd whine and she'd whine
till she whined herself shrill,
but that was just Bailey,
the dog with no chill.

Her school bus would come,
 and she'd drop her chew toy,

 run right to the door,
 and start jumping for joy.

She'd hop on the bus
and then whine the whole way.

When she finally got there,
it was time to play!

She darted in circles,
   and dove around bends,
      and dashed back and forth
         with all her puppy friends.

She raced in the grass,

and she dug in the dirt,

and she ran and she ran
till her little feet hurt.

But she wouldn't sit down
and she wouldn't sit still,
cause that was just Bailey,
the dog with no chill.

Soon, back she would come, muddy from head to toe,

and right from the door to the bath she would go.

Then what came next
was her least favorite part,
when the soaping
and washing
and scrubbing
would start.

Getting clean in the tub was just boring and lame...

But catching the bubbles
was a pretty
fun game!

She chased after them
as the shampoo made more,
and she splish-splashed
so much that she flooded
the floor!

You'd think after all that
she'd sleep like a log,
but Bailey was
one crazy un-lazy dog!

She'd run to the left, and she'd dodge to the right, and then hide your stuff under the bed out of sight.

She'd take anything, anything you might use, from papers and pencils to buttons and shoes!

Where is my left sock?
We may never know.
Only Bailey can tell us
where all these things go.

She hid my hairbrush,
she buried my ball,
then she took the tissues
and ran down the hall.

She was ripping them up
just as fast as she could,
but soon her mum caught her
and made her be good.

With that, the fun ended, and right about then, her lack of chill would start to come out again.

She whined cause she wanted to go out and play. Cause unlike her humans that stayed in all day...

She loved to play rowdy,
and loved to play rough,
and she was pretty tough
for a little white puff.

She'd pull on your sock, and she'd untie your shoe,
and she'd squeak any squeaky toy
that she could chew.

She'd grab at your feet,
and she'd nip at your hands,
and she'd pull on your sleeves
and then tug on your pants!

Soon with all her whining
and playing too rough,
her mum decided,
enough was enough!

"No! No, little dog!
You are being a pill!
You can't nip and whine
and take things as you will!"

But all of those times,
they were fun as could be...

"The dog with no chill
couldn't really be me."

She thought and she thought
and thought even more still,

"Am I really the dog
with no chill?"

Between playing and yipping
and nipping and such,
maybe it was just
a little too much.

If she caused a stir,
she had to be sure
it was fun for everyone
and not just her.

Still, Bailey just wanted
to play all the more,
and wanting to play is quite
hard to ignore.

She tried not to whine,
but not whining is hard.
She wanted to go out
and play in the yard!

But there was one thing
she knew meant even more,

for she was a dog
with more chill
than before.

So, she patiently sat

like a good ball of fluff,

waiting until her human had finished their stuff.

Then after the running
and having of fun,
she knew that the time now
for playing was done.

So, she hopped into bed without making a peep, snuggled up to her human and went off to sleep.

Then just for a moment,
things were quiet and still...

and that's how the dog, Bailey,
got a little more chill.

ABOUT THE DOG: THE BI-DOGRAPHY

This book was based on a true story and a real dog. Here are some fun facts about the real-life Bailey!

- Bailey's full name is Bailey Button Mariolis and she is a Bichon Frise.
- She was the runt of her litter and was 2.5 pounds when she was adopted. She was so small as a puppy that she had to play with cat toys because regular dog toys were too big.
- Bailey couldn't climb stairs until she was almost six months old. She would just whine to be carried up and down.
- Bailey's puppy school friends in this book are based on her real-life puppy friends. Their names are Cida the Corgi, Amber the Collie, and Charlie the Yorkie-Mix. The dogs get picked up in the morning by a real-life doggy school bus!

- Bailey's rubber duck was her first ever Christmas present from Santa and it is one of her favorite toys to play with (outside of the bath).
- Her favorite hobbies are chasing chipmunks and stealing socks from the laundry.
- In her free time, she also enjoys ripping up toilet paper and rubbing herself on the couch until her fur stands up from static charge.

- Bailey was less than a year old at the time this story was written, she was 2 by the time the book was finally published.
- Bailey chewed through multiple pages of the rough draft during the writing of this book.

THE AUTHOR

Elise Mariolis is a newly established author and one of Bailey's primary humans. She studied mathematics at WPI for several years but has since decided to take up more creative endeavors, like this book. She currently lives in Massachusetts with Bailey and her family.

Don't forget to check out our website for more awesome Bailey content!

dogwithnochill.com

THANK YOU!!

This book was only possible thanks to the generous donors that funded our Kickstarter campaign. We never could have published this book without the help of their selfless contributions. Thank you to all our supporters for making this dream a reality!

THE BIGGEST BELIEVERS IN THIS PROJECT WERE:

Chuck and Tara Mariolis, Kleon and Maria Giavasoglou, Rina Bell, Don and Nancy Smith, Cheryl and Daisy Mariolis, Lauren Mariolis, Noodle and Mala, Abby Burke, and our friends from New England Volleyball.

ISBN: 978-1-7377033-1-0
Printed in PRC